This Book Belongs to:

_____

Name

For my grandsons Matt and Jake.
Special thanks to their parents, aunt and uncle
who brave long trips to bring three
generations together.
(especially Philadelphia to Princeville)

The Giggles Group

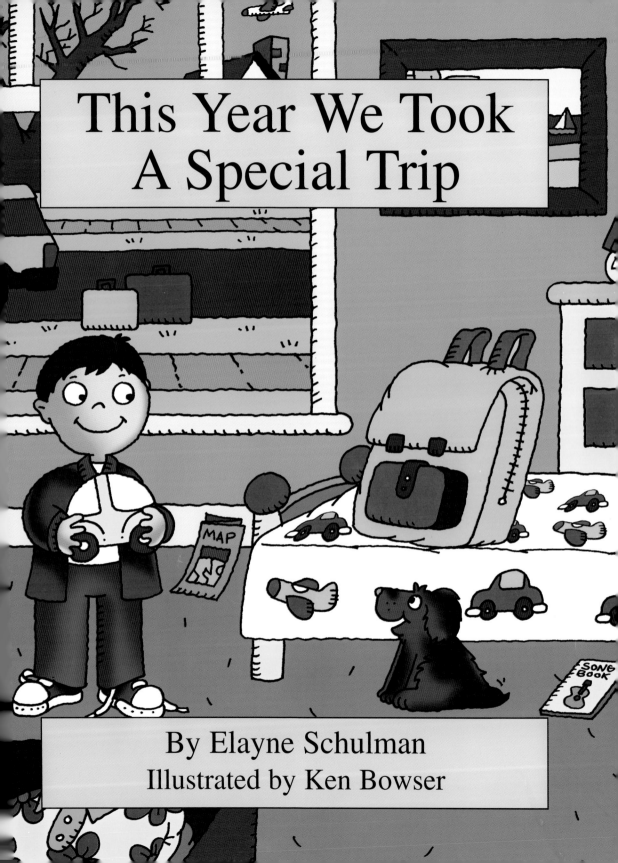

This Year We Took
A Special Trip

By Elayne Schulman

Illustrated by Ken Bowser

This year we took a special trip,
    A really big surprise.
Mom packed a map and special stuff.
    Dad tucked in shorts - no ties!

My toys couldn't fit in just one bag.
    They filled up more than two.
Snacks and games and books and tapes.
    I had a backpack, too!

Dad washed the car and cleaned it out.
        Stopped the mail and all.
"Shut the windows, and close the house.
        Take what you want. Last call."

We hauled the bags and stuffed the car.
        I didn't think it would all fit.
I carried snacks and pulled my wheels.
        We almost couldn't sit.

"Oh, getting there is half the fun."
I've heard that said before.
But being there's the better half,
Because someone's at the door!

On the road we sang silly songs.
  We watched as things went by.
"Wheels on the bus go round and round."
  The train just seemed to fly.

Hustle - bustle on all the roads;
  Taxis in the fast lanes.
People headed to work or play
  Waved from the cars and trains.

"Are we there yet?" I asked again.
The plane was on our right.
We unloaded all our bags and
They moved right out of sight.

We waved goodbye to puppy, too.
He's off now. Wonder where?
The car was parked and left behind.
Our plane was waiting there.

"Oh, getting there is half the fun."
I've heard that said before.
But being there's the better half,
Because someone's at the door!

I sat right in the window seat
   And watched the clouds go by.
Shaving cream and whipped cream clouds.
   I wished that I could fly.

On the plane they gave us lunch,
   A special meal and things.
They treated us so very nice.
   We even got some wings!

I had a blanket - pillow, too.
    I was a sleepy head.
I had to take a nap just then
    And dozed as Mommy read.

A pleasant thought was in my dream,
    I'd help to fly the plane.
I'd get us there in half the time,
    Through even clouds with rain.

"Oh, getting there is half the fun."
    I've heard that said before.
But being there's the better half,
    Because someone's at the door!

I'd steer and turn and take control
    And safely bring us down.
I'd be a flying tiger ace,
    A hero round the town.

I'd be carried down the aisles
    As if I'd won a race.
Parades would drive me through the town
    To a very special place!

The sun was bright, sky all around,
But wait that isn't sky!
It's water all around the deck
And boats with sails so high!

We made it here while I had slept,
All safe and snuggled in,
Smiles and hugs are passing round,
From neighbors and our kin.

Oh, getting there **was** half the fun.
I've heard that said before.
But being there's the better half,
Because *family's* at the door!

Trip Glossary

 backpack

 baggage

 boat

 bus

 car

 cloud

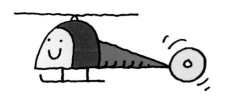 helicopter

 map

 meal

 plane

 puppy

 taxi

 train

 truck

 sailboat

 songbook

 suitcase

 wings

 wheels